ALSO BY ZUNI BLUE

Ninja Poo Gets Revenge
The Mean Girl Who Never Speaks
The Missing Hamster Who Didn't Escape

ZUNI BLUE

WHEN SNOW MEN ATTACK

ALL-SEEING BOOKS

LONDON

First published in 2013 by All-Seeing Books
www.all-seeingbooks.com

Cover Photo Copyright © MisterElements/bigstockphoto.com

ISBN-13: 978-1494411817
ISBN-10: 1494411814

CONTENTS

This book is written in British English.

When Snow Men Attack

"It's snowing!" Mum would shout upstairs. "Come see!"

We'd race downstairs to look outside. Of course we knew she was telling the truth, but we had to see it ourselves.

And there it was...

Slowly at first, and so few flakes. All different patterns, from the complicated to the simple. Hard snow on the ground, soft snow on top. We were so grateful to have a garden. It had *our* snow. No one else could have it.

If we were lucky, there'd be a day or two before the sun ruined our fun. Then the slippery, scary black ice would set in. But the snow was worth it.

But not to *everyone*.

"Mum? Dad?" I'd say. "Coming out?"

They'd shake their heads.

Not again!

I didn't understand why they never came out to play when it snowed. Why didn't they join our snowball fights? Why didn't they help build a snowman? Did they know how amazing it felt to make a snow angel?

How could they resist the snow?

I didn't know then.

I know now.

If I told you, would you believe me? Well, we're about to find out...

It was a cold Saturday morning. When the D-twins woke up, they expected the day to be like any other weekend - hours of bland homework followed by hours of fun. After writing an essay, finishing the annual cress seed project, and learning more complicated maths equations, they'd finally be free to play video games - that was Dixon - and reorganise doll collections - that was Daria.

But this wasn't just any Saturday. This was the Saturday when THE battle between snowmen and kids took place.

But excuse me for jumping ahead...

"Dixon!" their mum called from downstairs.

He groaned and pulled the covers tighter around his body, shivering at the thought of getting out of bed. It was times like this when he regretted having the room at the back of the house. It was the coldest in the winter and like a sauna in the summer.

"Yeah, Mum?" He lifted the cover off his head to hear her response. It would be an order to get downstairs and do more chores - yes, he was still being punished for the Ninja Poo incident - or just an order to get up.

"Daria!" his mum yelled. "Come down. Bring Dixon with you."

Daria burst in, fully dressed in a jumper and jeans. She had her pink boots on and his blue boots in her arms.

"Leave me alone," he mumbled. "No more poo!"

The smell of poo was long gone, but they were still finding poo stains weeks after Ninja Poo's defeat. Then his mum would enforce a boots-only policy until all the stains were gone.

"Where is it?" he asked. "Under the stairs? In Mum's rosebushes? On the cars?" He rubbed his eyes and yawned. "Not in the toothbrush pot again..."

Daria grinned. She pulled out her puffy, afro pigtails and plaited them neatly before tying them back into a bun.

That was unexpected. Daria didn't wear a bun unless it was a special occasion like ballet classes, swimming or--

"Snow!" Dixon said, so happy he almost cried. He ran to the window and threw open the curtains, his jaw dropping when he saw outside.

White. Perfect white. He couldn't tell where the white sky met the white houses. And it was still snowing, like a mini blizzard. There were paw prints across the garden, but the snow quickly filled the holes.

"How much time?" Dixon asked.

"It has been snowing for at least three hours." She glanced at her watch. "I didn't tell you earlier because the sun came out and could've melted the snow."

"It still might! Hurry!" He ran over the bed and charged downstairs. "I owe Jimmy for that sneak attack last year!"

He threw open the front door and stepped outside. The snow was so thick it reached just above his ankles. Shivering, he trudged to the pavement, but only reached the front gate.

"Dixon Davis," his mum snapped. "Have you gone mad?!"

"But--"

"You're still in your pyjamas! And barefoot! And you haven't even brushed your teeth!"

He closed the door before the neighbours heard.

An hour later, he was back. It only took that long because their mum made him put on three layers of clothing. Wearing a vest and pants, leg warmers and fleece, and a winter coat with baggy trousers, he could barely walk. By the time he reached the front gate, he was sweating. Daria was nice enough to dab his face with a snowball.

"Hurry up!" Daria said. "The good snow is at the park."

All the kids knew the park was the place to be. The snow in the street would be gone real quick, but there was enough snow in the park to last all day.

Dixon waddled faster while Daria skipped along. She wasn't wrapped up like him. His mum said it was because he'd gone out barefoot, so there was more chance of him catching a cold.

Yeah, right, he thought.

It usually took five minutes to reach the park down the street. Today it took fifteen minutes. So many times he'd been tempted to give up.

"It'll all be gone," he said. "Go without me. No point in us both missing it!"

"We're a team." She took his hand and pulled him along. "I can't be a team by myself."

Finally, they arrived. There were no more miles of freshly cut grass, clusters of trees with noisy birds or dogwalkers running around with their pets. Instead the scene was a pure white park with snowflakes raining down. The blanket of snow was so thick that it came up to his knees.

Usually the park was peaceful, empty. Besides Sam's howling and barking, nothing else made a sound. The busy traffic on the main road would fade away, the birds would stop chirping, and sometimes even Sam might sit still so he could take in the peace.

But not on a snow day...

Snowballs were flying. It didn't matter if they hit the intended target. As long as they hit someone, no one cared. Hiding behind the trees were at least ten girls, all armed with two snowballs each. Every few seconds, a girl would peek out. Dixon would've warned them the enemy was approaching from behind, but the enemy was a group of twenty boys.

And Dixon knew which side he was on.

Some kids went solo - they were sneakers. They slid over the snow in white camouflage. No one saw them until they threw a snowball. By then it was too late. Then the sneaker would sink back into the snow, gone without a trace.

Away from the snowball fights were lots of snowmen. It was a mutual agreement. The fighters stayed away from the snowmen, and the builders didn't build on the battlefield. If a snowball accidentally hit a snowman, the fighters rushed over to help rebuild.

Daria pulled off his coat and trousers. He spread his arms and fell backwards into the snow.

"Ouch!"

"What?" he asked, sitting up.

"I never said anything," Daria said. She waved over her friends. The trio sat on the snow, giggling. When Dixon went over, the girls gave him a cold stare.

"Girl talk," Daria said. "Bye, Dixon!"

He didn't mind. He hadn't come to giggle over someone's diary. He was here for more serious matters like building a snowman.

Dixon ran to the edge of the park and looked around for a good spot. Most kids just built anywhere, but he knew better. The best spot to build was in the middle so the other snowmen could be a wall of defence.

But defence from what?

First, the animals.

The smallest threat was the birds. They liked swooping down to peck at the juicy carrot noses. Some really bold birds tried to take the bag of carrots with them, but luckily it was too heavy. It didn't stop them from trying, though. When the kids heard a squawk and saw a shadow overhead, the builders had seconds to duck.

The biggest threat was the dogs. If they were vegetarians, they'd jump up and snatch the carrots. Some large dogs just took the whole bag, and growled if anyone chased them, so the kids just let it go.

I don't like carrots, Dixon always thought. Take 'em.

But carrot snatching was nothing.

For some reason, no dog could resist peeing on a snowman. It's like they knew that snowman took hours of work, but just didn't care. Dixon could've sworn that Sam was smiling when he peed all over his snowmen, and Sam was never sorry about it. Instead of rolling over in apology, he'd run circles around the snowman sizzling away in his warm pee.

Second reason to build his snowman in the middle was to keep it safe from Mother Nature. She was bossier than his real mum! Mother Nature sent strong winds that blew carrots, hats and scarves off. Then she'd send rain to wash away the snow. England was usually cold, but the one time everyone liked the cold - on snow day! - Mother Nature turned up the heat. How? The sun!

This was the last reason why Dixon built the snowman in the middle of the group. At sunrise and sunset, the sun would be on one side or the other. Any snowman in the middle could hide in the others' shadows.

This strategy meant Dixon's snowman always lasted the longest. The other kids could never figure out his secret, and he never told them.

So, Dixon started building. First he gathered the snow to make a large, round body. He ran to the forest and brought back two twigs for arms. They were sturdy, not too big or small, and branched off at the ends like little fingers.

"Almost done."

He gathered a smaller pile of snow and rolled it into a ball. He huffed and puffed as he lifted the head onto the snowman's body. When it was firmly on top, he flopped down into the snow, gasping for air.

Someone mumbled something. He sat up and looked around, but the other builders were busy tidying their snowmen.

He looked to the snowman.

Could it be...Nah! he thought. Don't be silly! They can't talk...

He laughed, but his sweaty hands were trembling. He shrugged off the mumble, but his heart kept pounding faster than usual. He got up to walk away, but didn't want to turn his back on the snowman.

"Hey!" Daria shouted. She skipped over the snow and stopped beside him. "Aren't you forgetting something?"

The great spot, strong branches for arms, smooth sides so it wouldn't catch the wind, and...

"His face," she said, her brown nose turning pink. "How can he talk to the others with no mouth? How can he see who he's talking to with no eyes? How can he respond if he has no ears to hear what they're saying?" She sneezed.

"I'll do it tomorrow." He took her hand. "You got a cold?"

She nodded, snot trickling from her nose.

"Home time."

"It's only been two hours!" She looked up at the clear, white sky. "The sun might come out soon."

"If the snow's gone tomorrow..." He shrugged. "Too bad."

Daria kissed his cheek and ran ahead. He blushed, even though no one was looking. And he felt a bit guilty.

He wasn't taking Daria home because he cared. He knew that if she got sick, he'd have to do her chores AND his. Plus she'd get time off school, which meant no homework for her.

"Not fair," he said. "Not fair."

He pulled off his vest and tore strips off. Then he tied them together and wrapped them around the snowman's neck.

"I'll bring you a face tomorrow," he whispered, "if you're still around."

"Hurry up," Daria shouted. She sneezed three times in a row and fell over.

"Gotta go!"

*

Dixon leapt out of bed and threw open the curtains. His eyes widened at the thick blanket of snow still over everything. He put his hands together and thanked Mother Nature for letting his snowman live to see another day.

"He'll have the best face in London...England...No. The world!"

After a quick shower, he rushed downstairs and rummaged through the kitchen cupboards. He grabbed a plastic bag and packed it with two carrots - one for back-up - a pack of juicy raisins, and an apple. The apple was a snack.

He'd need the energy. Today he'd spend the rest of the day making his snowman the best in the park. With his dad's sports cap and a proper woolly scarf - a Christmas gift he hated - he could make the snowman look cooler than everyone else's.

He ran out the front door and sped up the street. His arms and legs pumping, he moved faster and faster. Even when his legs were aching, and his jumper was stuck to his sweaty back, he didn't stop until he reached the park.

There was a large crowd of kids in his way. He couldn't see over their heads, so he got down on his hands and knees and crawled through.

"Why?" a girl cried, her coat stained with her tears. "I really liked that snowwoman. And they took my scarf too!"

He was curious, but he wasn't stopping now. He crawled faster, dragging the bag behind.

"I bet the park attendant did it," a teenage boy said, cuddling his little sister. She sobbed into his coat. "We'll build it at home next time, okay?"

Now Dixon started to sweat harder, but it wasn't because of the snow in his way. It was the amount of kids crying. Some just stared ahead, their faces blank. A few were shouting and kicking up snow. Then a fight broke out, but it wasn't serious. Two three-year-olds grabbed a hold of each other and wouldn't let go.

"Let's go home," a boy said. "Party's over."

Dixon broke free from the crowd and his jaw dropped when he saw the park. He rubbed his eyes and looked again, but the horror was the same.

"But, how?" he whispered. "Just yesterday..."

The park had been packed with snowball fights. There were walls of snow both teams had used as shields. All over the park were deep trails left behind by sneakers, snow angels where their targets had fallen.

Most importantly, there had been at least fifty snowmen. He closed his eyes and remembered the smart hats, sports caps, silky scarves, woolly scarves, scrawny carrots, chubby carrots, shrivelled raisins and juicy ones. Thinking back, it was like a crowd of villagers.

But they'd all moved on.

It was all gone.

All of it.

There were no hats and scarves on piles of melted snow where snowmen had stood. No holes where animals had dug up any food left behind.

It was all gone.

All of it.

The park was still covered in snow, but it was smooth, even, like no one had been there only twelve hours ago.

Woof! Woof!

Sam ran past and shot across the park. Dixon sprinted after him, spilling his carrots and raisins on the way. He dropped the bag and chased Sam into the woods.

"Sam! Stop!"

Sam stopped, but only long enough for Dixon to catch up. Then Sam's ears pricked up and slowly turned towards the lake. When Dixon tried to grab his collar, Sam dashed to the lake.

Dixon didn't follow straight away. It was getting dark, even though the morning sun had just come out. The deeper he moved into the forest, the thicker the tree branches overhead. Soon they blocked out the sky, leaving him in darkness.

In the distance, Sam was barking like crazy, but Dixon couldn't see him anymore. Close by, it was silent, but for Dixon breathing. He tried to breathe quieter, but then his heart started racing.

Alone in the dark, he felt someone watching. He crouched down so they couldn't see him, but the feeling didn't go away. Instead the feeling got stronger until he wanted to cry.

Someone was behind him. Their feet stepped on dry leaves, making them crackle.

"Go away!" He spun round, but no one was there. Then he looked down and saw Sam smiling at him, his tail wagging happily.

Woof! Woof!

Sam ran off again, but slower this time. Dixon followed. He had to. If his parents found out Sam had escaped because Dixon left the door open, he'd be in serious trouble.

So, he followed.

Around ten minutes later, he stepped out of the forest. He'd never been so happy to see the sun.

Sam crouched down and crept ahead, his ears slowly turning ahead. They fixed on the lake, so Dixon looked ahead.

He couldn't believe his eyes.

*

Typical, Daria thought. Sleeping late, as usual...

She couldn't understand why her parents were so lazy on Sunday mornings. Monday to Friday, they'd jump out of bed at 6 a.m. Come Sunday, she'd have to drag them downstairs for breakfast.

Daria closed their door and returned to her room. She pulled on the especially fluffy, pink dressing gown that she saved for the days she got sick. Then she put on her even fluffier slippers and slowly went downstairs.

"Dixon?" she called downstairs. A breeze blew over the stairs. That's when she saw the front door was open a crack. Shivering, she closed it and went into the living room.

Suddenly a bad feeling rushed over her. She hated those.

"Dixon, wherever you are, be careful."

She sat on the sofa and looked outside. The sun slipped behind a dark cloud that stretched across the sky. Whenever a ray of light tried to break through, the cloud sucked it back in.

"After the booger king and ninja poo, it can't get worse...can it?"

*

The fifty snowmen were sitting on the frozen lake. In the centre was a tall snowman with muscular-looking twig arms. Hanging loosely from his neck was Dixon's torn vest.

"That's my snowman," Dixon whispered. "He's the leader. So cool!"

He crawled closer with Sam. To camouflage with the snow, he pulled snow onto his body and lay on his stomach. Slowly, he slid closer to the snowmen gathered in the middle of the lake.

Dixon's snowman opened his twig hand and ten snowmen rushed forward. They pulled off their raisin smiles and stuck them on his twig fingers. The leader stuck the raisins on his head and spread them into a frown.

The other snowmen, and one snowwoman, sat around the leader again. Dixon assumed their beady black eyes were on the leader.

"Welcome, dear friends," Dixon's snowman said in a deep, booming voice. It was so loud the lake shook. Dixon held on tightly until the lake was still. Sam whimpered and crawled back to land, leaving him behind.

"Scaredy cat!" Dixon snapped.

"I need eyes," the lead snowman said. "You! Now!" A small snowman at the front handed over his eyes and stumbled blindly back to his seat.

"Lady and gentlesnowmen," the leader began, "for too long our kind has suffered. No more!" He raised a twig fist and the group cheered. "We have been peed on, rained on, melted, lost our faces to animals, been left naked to the brutal elements of that horrible sun. No more!"

The crowd were on their "feet". They clapped their branch hands and cheered until the snowman raised his fist again. They sat down and waited in silence.

"We have been mistreated for too long. After all the joy we bring those pesky kids, how do they thank us?" He put a hand to his ear.

"They leave us outside!" the others shouted together.

"Exactly," the leader said. "They have a perfectly good fridge to store us in. Instead they let us melt away in pain year after year. No more!"

A dark cloud spread over the lake, and soon it was as dark as the night. Luckily the park lights came on, so Dixon slid closer to the edge.

"The time has come, dear friends. Today we will rise up and take over the coldest countries on earth." His head turned to Dixon. "Let's start with him, shall we?"

Dixon jumped up and ran faster than ever. He didn't get far. His foot slipped through the ice, which sealed around it. He tugged on his leg, but the ice was too strong.

The snowmen slid closer, gliding silently over the ice. Their black eyes narrowed as they edged closer, and their frowns turned up into smiles.

Dixon thumped the ice with his fists, but it hurt, so he stopped. He wriggled his leg to shake off his shoe- it worked - but before he could pull his foot free, the hole tightened on his ankle. It held him firmly in place.

The snowmen surrounded him and closed in. The leader's arms grew bigger, his twig fingers lengthening until they looked like claws.

"Sam!" Dixon shouted. "Help me!"

The snowmen closed in faster, sniggering.

Sam flew over the smallest snowman and slid across the ice. He peed on the ice, melting the trap on Dixon's leg. Then he barked and charged back to the small snowman. Dixon ran after him, trying not to slip.

The small snowman's eyes widened in fear. He looked to the leader, who rushed over.

But it was too late.

Sam knocked the small snowman's head off and Dixon piggybacked over the body. He fell off and lost his footing, landing on his bum.

Woof! Woof! Sam growled.

Dixon looked back and saw a tiny crack in the ice. It trickled closer like a river, before splitting apart. Then there were five rivers of icy water.

"Sam, run!" Dixon glanced back, but Sam was already halfway to land. "Wait for me!"

Dixon scrambled to his feet and ran. Every time he looked back, the cracks in the ice were bigger and wider and moving faster. Big blocks of frozen lake sank, leaving giant holes he could easily fall through.

But that wasn't the worst part.

Up ahead, safely on land, Sam was barking at the edge of the lake. When Dixon got closer, he saw the large gap spreading between the lake and park. This crack circled the border, cutting the lake off.

Crack. Crack. Crack.

Dixon put his feet down and skated on. He kept his body close to the ice, pushing down hard on his legs. His thighs worked harder the faster he slid, but he couldn't feel any tiredness. All he could feel was the cold.

There was a loud roar as the frozen lake broke away from the forest. The lake swayed like a boat on water, making Dixon feel sick. But he had to keep going. The cracks were tearing up the ice behind him, throwing up chilly water. Right behind the cracks were the snowmen, the leader's twig claws reaching out to Dixon.

"Run, Sam!" Dixon yelled, close to land. "Go home!"

Sam ran into the forest, barking all the way.

Dixon skated even lower, his eyes fixed on the forest. Willing the power in his skinny legs, he pushed off the ice and flew. The forest was so close yet so far. A five second flight felt like an hour. Panic set in. He wondered what would happen if he didn't make it. He could swim, but would the ice let him?

Thud!

Dixon fell flat on his face in the frosty mud. Dizzy, he wobbled to his feet and looked back.

The layer of ice on the lake fell apart, crashing into the water. The snowmen tried to grab a hold of the ground, but their fingers slipped away. One by one, they sank into the lake and faded away into the darkness.

"It's over," he said.

*

Daria's eyes were glued to the television. Onscreen was the latest Robin dollset. She came with a four bedroom house, six seater car, and an entire wardrobe full of some of the prettiest clothes. Even better, now you could change her hair! Daria couldn't wait to swap Robin's long, blonde hair for a curly, brown afro like her mum used to wear.

"I'll start planning right now," Daria said. "Why wait for Christmas?"

Daria was so busy planning each outfit Robin would wear that she didn't notice the thud outside. Well, actually she did notice. She just didn't care. If she had cared, she would've looked out the window and seen the snow falling off the houses. She would've seen the snow gathering together in the road, blocking off the end of the street. She would've seen flocks of pigeons flying away, families of foxes scattering into the back garden, and sheets of ice sealing the doors shut.

But she didn't see it because she didn't care, right now.

Not right now, but soon...

*

Dixon stepped out of the forest and trudged across the snow. The kids were still in the field, but now they were rebuilding the snowmen, and snowwoman. He shuddered, not from the cold but fear as he passed through the rows upon rows of snowmen. They towered over him, their dark eyes shifting slowly as he passed. But whenever he looked back, their eyes snapped back into place.

"Jimmy!" Dixon shouted.

"Here."

Dixon jumped from fright and spun round to face his neighbour. Jimmy's spotty face was as pale as snow, his eyes wide with fear. His gaze fell on Dixon's shoeless foot.

"Where's your shoe?"

"In the lake."

"You mad? Skating on frozen lakes is really dangerous. You could've drowned."

"Our snowmen were on the lake!"

Jimmy smiled. "Hey, everyone! Dixon found our snowmen." Jimmy led three cheers. "Who took 'em?"

"Nobody. They walked there themselves."

It was too late to take the words back. When he looked around, their faces were a mixture of "He's crazy!" and "He's really crazy!" and "Why's he got one shoe on in this freezing cold? Because he's really, really crazy."

"Ha!" Jimmy laughed. It sounded forced. "Good, um, joke."

Again, Dixon spoke without thinking ahead.

"I'm serious."

There were sniggers. Then laughter. Jimmy smirked and pulled his scarf over his smile.

"They attacked me!" Dixon cried.

"Why?" Jimmy asked.

"Because I saw their top secret meeting on how to take over the cold parts of the world. The leader tried to get me. The leader was my snowman I made yesterday."

Jimmy walked away, giggling behind his scarf. The others turned back to their snowmen.

A snowball flew past Dixon and smacked the back of Jimmy's head. It hit so hard he almost toppled over. Luckily an older boy grabbed his arm and held him up. His legs wobbly, Jimmy shuffled back to Dixon and glared at him.

"Cheap shot," Jimmy spat. "Not cool."

"It wasn't me!"

"It's not funny anymore." Jimmy rubbed the back of his head. "There could've been a stone in there or something."

"I didn't do it!"

Jimmy walked away again. He spun round just in time for another snowball to hit him in the face. This one was a stunner. He fell backwards, out cold.

"Attack!" a woman's voice screeched. Dixon turned and saw the snowwoman pull two more snowballs from the ground. With the flick of her twig wrist, the balls shot across the field, knocking out the two biggest boys. Before they hit the snow, she struck again. This time it was two teenage girls.

"Run!" Dixon yelled.

A row of trees in the forest toppled over. Out from the shadows appeared Dixon's snowman, the vest now a sling for his broken twig arm. His beady eyes shot an evil look across the field, hitting Dixon right between the eyes. Then his twig finger rose and pointed at Dixon.

"Leave him for me," he shouted. "Capture the rest...alive, for now."

The snowmen around them uprooted from the snow and towered over the children. Quickly surrounded, the children gathered together. Someone pushed Dixon to the front, just as the leader approached. Teeth chattering and frozen beads of sweat on his brow, Dixon still managed to stand tall.

I've beaten him before, he thought. That means I can do it again.

"Dixon," the leader hissed, "because you are my father, I'll let you have one last request before we doom mankind, you and your parents...So, boy, what'll it be?"

This time he thought before speaking. He thought of the snowmen taking over London, England, Britain, Europe...then the world. It would be World War Three! Humans versus Snowmen. If it was the summertime, people might've stood a chance, but, instead it was another bitterly cold, cloudy British winter. He looked up and willed the sun to come out. Instead it hid behind another dark cloud spreading across the sky. Soon it was as dark as the night sky, and chilly too.

The sun wasn't coming to their rescue.

He thought of Daria. Maybe their twin sense would kick in. She'd come to find out what was wrong. When she saw the evil snowmen, she'd call their parents. Then what? Then nothing. Their mum and dad hadn't believed them when the twins exposed Booger King and Ninja Poo. Typical for parents. It was like they'd forgotten what it was like to be kids.

Their parents weren't coming to his rescue.

Jimmy would have a plan, but he was still out cold in the snow. The older kids could've helped, but they were unconscious too. If the sun wasn't being such a scaredy cat, it could've helped.

Nope. The kids were on their own...or were they?

"Haven't got all day, boy!" The leader's twig fingers grasped Dixon's hair and pulled him closer. "Well?"

"Can I play fetch with my dog one last time?" He forced out a tear. "Just to say goodbye before you take over the universe."

"The universe, eh?" The snowman grinned. "I like the sound of that...Okay. One game and that's it."

Dixon cupped his hands to his mouth and cried, "Sam! Play fetch!"

Sam rushed over and skidded to a halt behind the snowmen. They edged away from him slightly when he lifted his leg to scratch off some fleas.

"Fetch!"

Sam leapt to his feet and whimpered. He looked around the ground. Then he raced off to the forest, so Dixon quickly called him back. Sam ran back, whimpering louder than before.

"Fetch!" Dixon shouted, his eyes motioning to the leader's arm. "Fetch!"

Sam leapt up and his jaws clamped down on the twig. The snowman yelped as the fingers released Dixon's hair. Dixon snatched the twig and threw it as far as he could. The leader slid across the snow but Sam reached the twig first. He ran off, the leader close behind.

The snowwoman shouted, "Forget the twig! What about these brats!"

23

"Woman, did you see that beautiful twig? So hard, not too dry or damp. Just perfect." An icy tear slid down the leader's cheek. "It was one of a kind."

While the pair argued, Dixon edged to the gap left by the leader. It was wider now the snowwoman had moved away. A nice gap at least three kids could squeeze through. But they had to be quick.

"Psst," Dixon whispered. "I need two volunteers."

Silence. No one moved.

"I can't do this by myself."

"I'll go with you." It was Jimmy. A big, red bump poked out of his scruffy, brown hair. "Sorry about earlier."

"Anyone else?"

The other kids backed away from the opening.

"Just you and me, then," Jimmy said. "They'll stay behind with the snowmen. We'll tell their parents what happened." He hugged some of the girls goodbye before returning to Dixon. "Poor kids. They don't stand a chance."

The boys edged closer to the opening. Dixon felt many pairs of eyes on him, but he was too scared to look. He kept his eyes to the ground and followed Jimmy.

"Dixon, no one likes being left behind...They'll run too. Trust me."

"But we won't all make it!"

"You don't have to be the fastest, just not the slowest."

Dixon looked back and saw fear on the kids' faces. Tears in their eyes. Snot in their noses. Their feet shifting closer, closer, closer.

"Get ready," Jimmy said. "Remember what I said?"

"Don't be the slowest."

"Count to three." The boys faced the opening. "One...Two...Three!"

Jimmy shot off like a rocket, but Dixon managed to keep up. A thunderous noise of kids stampeding after them followed close behind. It drew nearer as the kids ran faster and faster.

The snowwoman's head turned to the opening, but she was too late. The boys had already slipped through, a hundred kids right behind them. The snowmen rushed together, trying to block off the way out. A few kids were grabbed, the twig fingers caught in their clothes. The twig arms lifted, keeping the children off the ground. Some managed to wriggle free, but most could only cheer on Dixon and the rest from above.

"Fire!" The snowwoman shouted.

Snowballs shot across the park, knocking each kid down. Some jumped up and ran on only to be knocked down again. Others stayed down the first time, in tears as they rubbed their sore spots.

"Smaller balls," the snowwoman screeched. "More ammo!"

The fist-sized balls flew even quicker, several kids falling within seconds. The balls were so small they were quicker to make. The fallen children couldn't get back up because so many balls were flying by. The children lowered their heads in defeat and raised their hands.

But Dixon kept running. Every time he fell behind the rest, he moved faster until he was back in the middle of the group. He wished he could be at the front with Jimmy, but his legs were too sore. Gasping for air, he felt a bit of relief when the bottom of their street was in sight.

"Regroup!" the snowwoman ordered. "Our leader has returned."

Dixon knew he shouldn't have, but he slowed down to look back. Sam ran over, licked his cheek and raced after the others. He wanted to keep moving but the snowmen's next move had his attention.

The leader, whose favourite arm was back, jumped up and fell into the snow. His twig arms waved before slipping away. The other snowmen did the same, taking their clothes with them.

There was silence.

The other kids stopped running and started cheering. Only Jimmy kept going, not stopping until he was outside his house. That's when Dixon noticed the snow piled up in the road, not a single flake anywhere else.

"It's over!" a girl squealed.

"Uh oh..." Dixon's heart raced. "Here we go again."

The snow below his feet slid backwards, taking him with it. He jumped off and ran until he reached steady ground.

The snow whirled in the centre of field, dragging kids along for the ride. Round and round they were spun as the snow rolled together into a lump. Slowly the lump turned in a pile of snow the size of a sports car. More snow was sucked in until it was the size of Dixon's house. Then twig hands popped out of the snow and rubbed the snow, smoothing it down into a giant snowball.

Dixon thought of the giant booger ball when Booger King had attacked. He could've eaten his way out, but he couldn't do that with snow.

There was only one option.

"Run!" he yelled. "Go home. Lock yourself in!"

Everyone ran down the street, looking out for their house. When the park was clear, Dixon ran home. Their house was halfway down the street. Even with the street packed with kids, he could get home easily, but then snow wrapped around his feet and held them down. He screamed for help, but no one came but Sam.

"Go home, Sam! Get help!"

Sam licked Dixon's cheek before running home.

"I don't think I'll make it outta this one," he said to himself. He closed his eyes and pictured Daria and his parents and Sam. He wondered how she'd cope when she wasn't a twin anymore. "Oh boy..."

*

Daria couldn't ignore that scream. She looked out the window and saw kids running home. First she thought it was going to rain - the dark cloud was still looming over their street - but then the cars outside started shaking, and a few alarms went off. Then the living room trembled too, shaking pictures off the walls. She ran into the doorway, just as they had during their first, and only, earthquake.

Then the floor was still.

"What on earth?" She clung to the door frame, her feet glued to the spot. "Do we have earthquakes in England? I thought that was just America and Asia and--"

Bang bang! Someone was at the front door. She peeked through the letterbox and smiled. Jimmy didn't smile back. In fact, he looked like he was going to cry. No one had ever seen Jimmy cry, so things had to be serious.

"It's Dixon," he said. "I think they've got him."

"Who?"

"The snowmen."

She opened the door and let him in.

"Did you hear me? Snowmen took 'im!"

"After Booger King and Ninja Poo, snowmen are nothing! Yes. I heard you. Yes. I believe. Yes. This means war."

She ran upstairs and got changed into her warmest coat, thickest boots, and wrapped up tight in her hat, gloves and scarf. When she returned downstairs, Jimmy was peeking out the letterbox.

"What's the matter?" she whispered.

He waved her over, so she looked outside. The snow in the road had spread across the front garden and frozen the door. Now it wouldn't open, no matter how hard they both tugged.

"We're stuck," Jimmy said. "I'd go upstairs but that's a loooooong drop."

"Where's Dixon?"

"At the park."

"We're going there. Get ready."

"What?!" Jimmy cried. "How can we fight?"

"You know everyone who lives on this street, correct?"

"Yep. So?"

"Call the kids. Tell them we're breaking out. Then we're going to war." She clenched her fists, her angry eyes staring ahead. Then she glared at Jimmy and said, "Well? Get to work! The phone's by the sofa. Move it!"

Daria went into the kitchen. It smelt of coffee, so her parents were awake. Steam was still flowing out of the kettle, so they'd just woken. Coffee woke them up, her dad said. He couldn't think without it.

Daria wished she was allowed some. She hadn't told Jimmy, but she was terrified. She had no ideas, and knowing all the kids would expect results was pressure she wished she didn't have.

"If I can't have a coffee, I'll have a cold drink instead."

She tipped ice cubes into a glass and reached for the taps. Without thinking, she filled it with hot water. The ice cracked and creaked as it melted away. Soon it was tiny pieces of smooth ice floating like icebergs in the ocean. A grin on her face, she watched as the last pieces turned into water.

"I have an idea..." She turned to the kettle. "Let the battle begin."

*

His real name was Sid.

He was at least a hundred years old. He had no idea when he'd been born. All he knew was that this year would be different from the others. No more melting in the sun. No more being peed on by dogs.

27

No more salt making his snow feet sting. He didn't have to fear the sun ever again. With his loyal followers, he'd take over not only the world but the universe.

And it all started with taking over Dixon and Daria's street.

That's where the giant snowball came in.

He was going to roll it down the street, sucking in anyone in his way. As he gathered more snow along the way, soon he'd be so big that the ball couldn't fit in the street. Too bad for the humans. His snowball would roll over cars, houses, supermarkets, zoos and everywhere else. Then the humans would be begging him for mercy. Too late for them.

The world would be his, well, most of it. Hot places like Jamaica and India would still be off-limits, but who wants ugly beaches when you can have miles upon miles of white snow and ice in the North and South Poles? Sid couldn't wait to ski and ice skate, and walk with polar bears, and play with penguins, and dive to the bottom of an iceberg, and moonbathe on the coldest spot on earth.

Deep within that giant snowball, Sid was dreaming of his own igloo home. That's why he did nothing when he spotted the kids breaking out of their homes. In fact, he turned away and took his eyes off so he could dream better. That's why he didn't see the kids carefully pouring boiled water down the front of their houses, but he felt a tiny bit of pain when the hot water melted the ice. He didn't see Dixon's sister, who was technically Sid's aunt, lowering herself into the front garden on a cord. He didn't see the hairdryer at the end.

And all he had to do was put on his eyes.

But he didn't see it because he didn't care, right now.

Not right now, but soon...

*

"Freeze!" Daria shouted. She pointed the hairdryer at the snow on the front gate. It formed two snow hands and raised them up. "Move and I'll shoot!"

"Don't!" the snow squeaked. "What ya want?"

"We need a wall, but the snowmen can't know."

The snow formed an eyebrow and raised it. "A detachment? Easy peasy...Not doin' it. Sorry."

"Why not?"

"Sid'll get us! He's taking over the world, I heard. Best be on his team, ya know?"

She turned on the hairdryer, but only the cool setting. Even that was enough to make the snow cower behind its hands. It formed an eye that peeked out. She placed a finger on the setting button and slowly pushed it over to the middle setting. The air turned warm, making the snow around her slide away.

"Okay! Okay!" The snow hands clasped in prayer. "We'll detach...but only if we get another day."

"You can sleepover in the freezer for as long as you like, okay?"

They shook hands.

"He'll know when we detach. He'll come looking for us...and you." The snow shuddered. "Whatever you're doing, do it quick."

The snow closed its eye and twitched. The ground trembled, knocking Daria over. She grabbed the fence and clung on until the earthquake passed. A minute was all it took, but to Daria it felt so much longer.

"All done!" the snow said. "We'll do whatever you want."

Daria gave Jimmy the thumbs up. From her bedroom window, he waved at the other houses. The ice blocking each door fell away and the other kids ran out. They huddled outside Daria's house. She climbed onto the front wall to address them.

"Sorry, but we don't have time for a pep talk. Let's get down to business." She pointed at the wall of snow at the end of the street. "Builders, listen! When I say so, build another wall at the other end. Make it high and as thick as possible. If the snowmen make it over, be ready for a fight. Right now, build really, really high walls on both sides of the street. Make sure there are holes to jump out, but not too big or the snowmen will escape."

The twenty-four builders nodded before running off to work.

"Sneakers, blend with the walls. Make sure you're not spotted or everything will be ruined."

The six sneakers nodded and slipped away. Daria blinked and each sneaker had vanished.

"The rest of us are fighters." She raised her fist and the hundred others did the same. "I know you are scared," she said, her voice trembling, "but Dixon helped you lot. You owe him."

The kids' heads hung in shame and their shoulders drooped.

"Don't feel too guilty. Feel brave. Feel strong. Feel fear and fight anyway!"

The crowd cheered.

"Get extension cords, hairdryers, heaters, salt, balloons, leftover water in the kettle, and bring your dogs and rabbits." They looked confused. "Just do it. It'll make sense later..."

*

The giant snowball would barely fit down the street, but that didn't matter. It had to be that large to fit one hundred snowmen inside and keep out any sunshine. The cowardly sun was still hiding behind the clouds, but Sid could never tell when it might peek out. Even one ray of light hurt, so it was safer to stay out of sight.

But soon the sun wouldn't be a problem.

Nighttime was coming. That meant it'd be bedtime soon. When the parents took their children in, the battle would be over. No one would believe the kids until it was too late. By then, Sid and his army would have control over Britain. Europe would be next. Then the world.

"Ready?" Sid yelled. The snow soldiers raised their twig fists in the air. "I can't hear you!"

"Yes sir!"

"Remember, just distract them long enough for nighttime. Then we'll lock them indoors."

The soldiers stood in line. They took each other by the hand and looked straight through the ball. Ahead was the street where Dixon lived. Besides the cars, it was empty. There were no witnesses.

It was the perfect time to strike.

"Soldiers, charge!" Sid ran and the others followed. Slowly the ball moved, gradually gaining speed as the soldiers ran faster and faster. Like hamsters in a wheel, they ran on the spot while the ball moved on, gathering snow they rolled over.

The ball stopped at the top of the street. At the other end was a chubby girl sobbing. Sid squinted and grinned when he recognised a pretty pink bow on the girl's boot. It was like the one on snowwoman's head, but damp and muddy.

When the girl looked up, the tears were frozen to her cheeks. Her eyes widened when she saw the snowball, but she never ran. She screamed and screamed, but no one came to her rescue. Then she ran, but there were walls of snow on either side. Sid couldn't remember telling the snow to trap his aunt, but he'd reward them later with a nice promotion.

"Hello, Daria," he whispered. He reached into the snowball's wall and pulled out Dixon. He held the boy tightly against his body and pointed to Daria.

"Say goodbye to Auntie Daria." Sid raised his fist and the soldiers sprinted. He and Dixon held onto each other as they rolled downhill, breaking the speed limit. Soon the houses and cars they passed were a blur. Dixon's brown cheeks turned bright green. Even Sid felt a bit woozy. Still, he couldn't take his eyes off Daria. Any moment now they'd roll over her, sucking her into the ball. His second prisoner. One of billions to come.

So why was she smiling?

Out the corner of his eye, Sid spotted a flicker of movement. He saw a pair of angry eyes in the snow. A sneaker! Sid's eyes shifted to the sneaker's hand as it tore from the wall of snow. The girl was holding a white balloon full of something red. A light red. A familiar red. He'd seen it before, but he couldn't remember where.

The sneaker raised her hand and threw the balloon.

His body remembered, though. That's why his snow heart skipped a beat. His body trembled and his mouth turned into a frown. Then his mind raced through thought after thought, memory after memory, but being so old meant he had too many memories flooding his mind at once.

The balloon struck the ground and burst, tiny red grains flying out. They scattered over the snow. Sid watched the snowflakes melt away, leaving the red grains behind.

That's when he remembered where he'd seen it before. It was Winter 1928. He was silly enough to let his flakes form outside a house instead of the local park. When morning came he was trampled over by children rushing to school, a van parked on him, and then a cat did a poo on him.

But that was nothing compared to what happened next.

An old, seemingly harmless man came out of the house. He almost slipped on Sid, but luckily his walking stick held him up. The man returned home and reappeared with a plastic bag full of red grains.

He poured them all over the ground and spread them around with the stick. With a proud smile on his face, he went back inside.

Then the pain began.

Back in the present, Sid watched in horror as more sneakers burst from the snow walls. Bag after bag flew into the road, right where the snowball was about to roll. Sid turned back to the soldiers and yelled, "Stop! Stop! Stop!" but it was too late.

The snowball rolled over the salt. The snowmen screamed as the salt warmed their feet. They climbed up the walls to escape the salt eating the floor, but their weight was too much. The walls collapsed and the ball broke apart. Both halves slid down the road, still melting away in salt.

Sid threw Dixon over his shoulder and shouted, "Attack! Attack! Attack!"

The snow soldiers pulled snow from their bodies and threw at the sneakers, who quickly faded into the walls. When all sneakers had vanished, the snowmen turned to Daria. She winked at Sid, the smuggest grin on her face.

"Run!" Dixon said.

"First phase, defence!" she shouted. "Neutralise the enemy!"

Sid turned back in time to see children climbing out of the walls. Each boy was armed with a hairdryer on its maximum setting. Each girl had a halogen heater glowing in the darkness of early evening. The fifty or so children stood tall. He saw no fear in their eyes, no tears either. Just anger. Fury.

"Fire!" Sid ordered.

The snowmen threw snowball after snowball, faster than ever before, but the kids didn't run this time. They fired the hairdryers, turning the snowballs into harmless sludge. The sludge slid down their coats and plopped on the ground. It melted away before Sid could call the snow back.

The snowmen started throwing at the girls but they used the halogen heaters as shields. The snow started melting long before it hit the hot bulbs inside. As they warmed up, the heat from the bulbs spread further.

"Second phase, offence!" Daria barked. "Get ready!"

The girls lined up with the heaters and marched forward. Sid backed away from the orange glow of heat, but when he turned back the boys were advancing from the other side. The boys aimed the hairdryers at the snowmen, edging closer.

Boxed in, Sid's mind went blank as paper. He started sweating from the heat. He pushed his way to the middle of the group and watched in horror as his soldiers melted away. A few went crazy, throwing more snowballs until only their heads were left. Seconds later, the heads were puddles of cold water at his feet.

"Leave and never come back," Daria said. "We didn't do anything to you!"

"Never," Sid spat. "We won't go down without a fight." He raised Dixon overhead and put a snowball to the boy's scarf. "Back off or the kid gets it."

"But I made you," Dixon said. "Doesn't that make your daddy?"

The other snowmen giggled.

"Silence!" Sid hissed. "Daria, call off your soldiers."

"Or what?" She placed her hands on her hips.

"Or your brother's toast. Literally!"

Her eyes moved from the heaters blazing to the hairdryers blasting. Then she looked at Dixon, who was soaked in sticky sweat. He shook his head and said, "Just do it. End it, and hurry up. It'll be bedtime soon!"

Daria raised both hands and then lowered them down. The kids slowly lowered the weapons, placed them on the ground and walked away. Not a single one looked back. Not even Daria. In fact, she led them away as if she was in a hurry to go somewhere.

Silly brat, Sid thought. You didn't think that far ahead, did ya?

Sid brought Dixon closer and looked in his eyes.

"I win, you lose," Sid said. "That's what happens when snowmen attack."

"Um, Sid..." The small snowman tapped him on the back. "Your auntie's back."

Sitting on top of the wall was Daria. She tutted at Sid, the smug look back on her face.

"Third phase, offence!" she shouted. "Attack!"

Sid almost dropped Dixon from fright. Out of fifty, now only thirty snowmen remained. It was getting harder and harder for Sid to hide. If he lost control of his soldiers, they'd desert him. Then he'd be all alone.

"Sneakers!" a snowboy cried. "Over there!"

The others armed themselves with two snowballs each. Sid stayed in the middle of the group, staying out of sight. He could still see flashes of white camouflage when a sneaker slipped by, but they moved so fast. Too fast. By the time his soldiers threw a snowball, the sneakers had gone.

For several minutes the sneakers teased the snowmen. He saw flashes of red salt but, strangely to him, they didn't throw them. That's when he knew: they were a distraction.

"Look out," a snow soldier cried. "The heat monsters!"

Sid spun round and gasped. At the top of the street were twenty children with kettles, steam billowing from the spouts. The kids poured, sending hot water flowing down the street. It mixed with salt, a deadly combination, as gravity pulled it faster down the road.

"Run!" Sid shouted. "Run for your lives!"

The snowmen slid down the street as fast as they could. Sid could feel the hot steam on his heels, so he pushed over some soldiers. They knocked over others, all toppling like bowling pins. Their bodies slowed down the boiling river, but some streams found a way through. They were cooler by now, but still painful to the touch.

But Sid wasn't afraid.

All he had to do was reach the bottom of the street and turn the corner. Then he could run to safety. Any garden would do. As long as he found shelter before the morning sun, everything would be fine. He could hide for the night and gather another army tomorrow.

He pointed his twig finger to the wall blocking the way out. The wall stood firm. His eyes willed the snow to fall, letting him pass. The snowflakes ignored him. He roared at the snow standing in his way, but his soldiers ignored him.

The detached ones, he thought. They betrayed me.

Or not.

The wall crumbled, leaving the end of the street wide open. Now safety was only three cars away. He felt so relieved that he slowed down. The boiling rivers reached his toes, but they were cold by now, some streams slightly frozen. The snowmen sucked the icy water in to repair their wounds.

Sid should have run - the way out was within twig's reach - but he *had* to see Daria's sad face. He had to see the tears in her eyes when he slid away with Dixon.

But when he looked back, she was on the road, two salt balloons in her hands. A hundred children were behind her: boys, girls, builders, fighters, sneakers. Each child was armed with a weapon, everything from kettles to heaters to whistles. Sid raised an eyebrow at the whistle. For some reason, it made him nervous.

"This is your last chance," she said. "Say sorry, go back to the park, never bully us again...Oh, and give my brother back."

"Let me think about that..." Sid laughed and stuck out his tongue. "You little brat. Think you can order me about? Not a chance! Family or not, you can't talk to me like that."

"Is that a no, then?" Daria glanced at her watch.

"Yes. I mean no! I mean yes, that's a no."

"Sorry, Dixy," Daria said. "You'll thank me later...I hope." She cupped her hands and put them to her mouth. "Sam? Go to the toilet!" She blew her whistle.

Another girl did the same, but she called for "Jane".

Then a boy cried, "Timmy! Come get some carrots!"

One by one the children called their pets or blew their whistles. Sid found it quite amusing. What on earth could a cute bunny rabbit do to him? Then his gaze fell to his carrot nose and he gulped.

A dog howled in the distance as the full moon pushed out the sun. The ground trembled, the pitter patter of paws fast approaching. He heard panting, whimpering, bells jangling, and tiny whiskers twitching. His gaze turned to the opening, where the snow was sliding away. The detached snow slid away quickly. He willed them to come back, but the snowflakes ignored him.

Then Sam appeared.

The dog charged over and skidded to a stop beside Sid. When Sam lifted his leg, Sid leapt out of the way seconds before he was hit. The warm pee sprayed the snowboy and he melted away. The other snowmen ran, but the pets were there to meet them. Ten dogs raised their legs and sprayed. The snowmen turned yellow as they sizzled away.

The rabbits pounced, snatching the snowmen's noses. Sid wasn't too bothered by that. At least he couldn't smell the pee anymore.

Stray cats jumped the snowmen, taking their raisin eyes and buttons. Sid used Dixon as a shield to protect his face. The cats hissed in frustration.

"You want to leave?" Daria asked. "Fine. Go! But you are not taking our stuff. If we lose it we'll be in trouble!" She turned to the kids. "Grab your stuff! Quick! It's bedtime soon!"

The kids charged over and pulled off their hats, scarves, and any food the animals didn't want. Naked, the snowmen and snowwoman turned red with embarrassment. They tried to run but the hairdryers melted them away.

All Sid could do was watch as his army fell apart - literally. Hot water flowed beneath him, melting his feet. Slowly he sank into a puddle of his own melted snowflakes. Pee was spraying, cats were picking at raisins, rabbits were fighting over carrot noses, hairdryers blasted the last of Sid's soldiers, and the heaters made the leftover puddles evaporate. Within minutes, Sid was the only one left.

He let Dixon go and raised his twigs in defeat.

The children cheered.

"Any last requests?" Daria asked, Sam sitting at her feet.

"Make it quick." Sid took off his eyes so he couldn't see what came next. "I deserve it."

He waited patiently. Would it be the hairdryer? Or maybe the halogen heater would melt him from head to toe? If the dogs' bladders had anything left, they'd waste it on him. He shuddered at the thought of the hot pee mixing with him in a smelly, yellow puddle. That's if the sneakers didn't blast him with more salt.

Instead, he felt a pair of soft hands clasp his twig hand. He popped in his eyes and looked at Dixon, who had tears in his eyes. The boy knelt in the freezing cold snow and bowed his head as Sid melted away.

"You really do...care about me...don't you?" Sid struggled to speak as his body melted away.

Dixon nodded, fighting back tears. Then one slipped out and landed on Sid's eye. It trickled down his round face and joined the puddle of snowflakes below.

"Sid, don't you get it? Course we care! Why'd you think we take ages building you every year? Why'd you think we give you our hats and scarves? Why'd you think we use food we could eat to build you a face? Sid, why'd you think we cry the day we find a puddle where you'd been? Because we care, that's why!"

It was getting harder to see, but Sid could make out the children's sad faces. The dogs were whining. The cats crying. The rabbits ran away. Daria was sobbing into her scarf. She knelt beside Dixon and took Sid's other twig.

"Will you come back?" Dixon asked. "It might snow next year!"

"Rematch?" Sid grinned.

"You betcha!" Dixon playfully punched Sid's cheek.

"I was wrong about you kids," Sid said. "Sorry. I just got fed up with missing out on so much. I wanted to be like you."

"Sid, you're missing out on fun, yeah, but boring stuff too like homework and chores." Dixon looked over his clothes and sighed. "I smell of wee! Mum's gonna kill me!"

Sid would've laughed if he still had a mouth. Instead he gently pulled his twigs free from the twins' hands and waved goodbye. The children waved back, some in tears.

"See you next year," Dixon whispered.

Bye Dad, Sid thought.

Just before he melted away, Sid looked to the sky as the sun peeked out from the clouds. A single ray shone on him, and then he was gone.

You never know when snowmen will attack. Some streets must battle every year. Some are lucky - their snowmen never fight at all. The fight might start at school, at work, at the park, at home, or on holiday...

No wonder Mums and Dads stay in. They're tired of fighting.

That's why the world relies on kids like you.

Only kids are quick enough to outrun snowmen. Only kids are small enough to wriggle free if they get caught. Only kids are smart enough to believe my story. By the time any adults believe me, it'll be too late.

So, the next time your older brothers and sisters and parents won't come out to play, you know why: They've retired from the Snow War. It's *your* turn now.

Oh, and give your pets a treat regularly. It doesn't matter whether you have a dog, cat, hamster, bird, sheep, cow or even a dragon. Stay on their good side. You never know when you might need help...

About the Author

Zuni Blue's been telling tales since she was a kid. Now she gets to mix fun stories with a few lessons learnt on the way to adulthood. Whether it's solving cases at school or fighting monsters, Zuni promises a great read you'll never forget!

Pen Names:
Zia Black www.ziablack.com (For Mums and Dads!)
Zhane White www.zhanewhite.com (For Mums and Dads!)
Zada Green www.zadagreen.com
Zuni Blue www.zuniblue.com

Dedications

Thank you to my family. I appreciate all the love and support you
have given over the years and in the future. Also, thanks to great
readers like you. Enjoy all my stories!

Printed in Great Britain
by Amazon

50395512R00026